BRAAMFONTEIN

(26.193°S 28.033°E)

———

Nongalaza kaNondela

BRAAMFONTEIN

Copyright © 2011 by Mnyandu Publishing

ISBN 978-0-620-46053-8

Printed in USA

The tragedy is that a generation of young men and women is growing up with the idea that junk sex is as good as it gets.

Tony Parsons

Chapter One

Those ones there you can fuck, said Jika in an assuring voice.

"Which ones," asked Chulo?

"Across the street dummy. Those ones, the one with Bermuda shorts. I know them; I used to fuck their roommate. Peep this!" Jika taps Chulo on his shoulder to get his complete attention, undivided attention.

"Peep this! Those females are whores. You can fuck there."

Late afternoon in Braamfontein, people are up and down. It's end of the day. Office *boys* and *girls* are rushing to their places of residence. Students from Wits University are up and about. Traffic on Jorissen Street is like shit. This is noise pollution at its best. This place, this city has changed a lot. It is no longer that famished-looking business area.

Last year they put up a Pick 'n Pay shop and got rid of OK shop. One in every three building is a student residential. The ABSA Bridge is gone, which was connecting Wits University with Braamfontein Centre. One hardly sees street kids and the homeless hanging around the Holy Trinity Chapel.

Chulo looks at Jika and says: "Why don't you call them and shit? You don't want to fuck?"

"Ofcourse, I do, shoo! A nice one like that, who wouldn't?"

The three females Jika was talking about were lazily walking across Jorissen Street right next to #66 Jorissen Place. They were going towards the Wits University direction. As they got to the robot at the intersection of Jorissen and Bertha, they turned right and crossed the robot to the other side of Jorissen and Jan Smuts, and made right again and they were now walking towards the Pick 'n Pay direction. Bitches, you'll never understand them sometimes. These one in particular, it's like they had planned the whole shit. It's like they were seducing the guys. They were very inviting.

"Yo son, they coming this way," said Jika. "Let's go chill by that Polo," said Chulo, pointing at Junior's car. Jika and Chulo quickly walk to the car and strike a pose. The females have lost the third one, they are now two. The females come and pass Jika and a frozen Chulo. No words came out from Chulo as females went pass them.

"And now," Jika asks?

"I didn't know what to say," says Chulo.

"Game is too big indeed hey, you even freeze when pussy comes crawling to you?"

"Fuck you man, let's go back to the rest of them fools." Jika and Chulo walk back to where the rest of them guys are.

It's a Friday afternoon, after work weekend fever is in the air. Traffic plagues Bertha, Jorissen, Jan Smuts, De Korte, De Beer, Melle, Biccard, Simmonds, Ameshoff, Loveday, Hoofd, Joubert, Harrison and Rissik. Music from cars and taxis is blurring. You can smell excitement and the mood is gay. There is something about this part of town that makes it exciting, interesting and appealing.

"What's the plan tonight," Punk asks?
"All I know is I wanna stick," says Chulo.
"Can it be a weekend without sticking?"
"Yeah! Can it be a weekend?"
"Yeah! It can, just not now or anytime soon."
"Why you sound like sticking is a crime? Sticking is good and all men need it.

Jika and Chulo walk to Pick 'n Pay in pursuit of those two females, no, in pursuit of that one female that Chulo hopes he might get. Jorissen Street is busy and inside Pick 'n Pay, it's packed, the afternoon rush.

It's a good thing that they finally opened up this Pick 'n Pay, Braamfontein was dead just like Lower Eastside Manhattan on a Sunday and you looking for some few groceries and shit.

Yesterday, corner of Braamfontein Centre and across where there used to be Chicken Licken, a body laid for hours without being attended to. The funny thing is, there were about two or three ambulances and some SAPS (South African Police Services) people but they were just standing there surrounding the body. Two, three hours later, the body was in a body bag, a red one. Finally, they decided to respect the dead. I was visiting this woman I wanted to stick on the 9th floor of BC (Braamfontein Centre) and I could see a group of people around the dead body. It was like they were having a memorial service (night vigil) for the body. I heard that it was a woman who had a heart attack, dropped and died. Damn - life is a bitch.

Those females that were at Pick 'n Pay the other day, I didn't fuck, fuck them. I passed her to my friend and I know he won't fuck coz he's a jerk.

Braamfontein is a nice place, a relaxed city. Should I call it a city or a residential area since there seems to be more residential blocks then office blocks. Everywhere you turn, a residential block, luxury apartments or soon to be luxury apartments.

An old White male I once met once said: "South Africa has gone to the dogs." I never bothered asking him why he said what he was saying because I believed that we are all entitled to our own opinions. Come to think about it, did Mandela sell us out to outsiders (foreigners), Americans, Brits, Chinese, Germans and stuff. I don't know or maybe I do know but not ready to admit it. Makes me question what is democracy if Kaffirs are still living broke. *Kanti* what were we doing April 27, 1994? Is this what we fought for, so that a few can be allowed to eat and the rest kept outside to catch crumbs. Jesus of the White men, what is going on? This religion nonsense is keeping us dumb and passive. We need to wake up like Samson with the Philistines, David with Goliath, Moses with Pharaoh, Daniel and The Three Young Men (Meshach, Shadrach and Abednego) with Nebuchadnezzar. Those guys stood up for their rights. We are definitely reading a wrong Bible when we don't realize that all the oppressed people had to stand up and fight, God didn't come down from the "heavens" and fought their battles. Miss me about Christianity; to me it looks like a social order that fears men but not God. The state killed Jesus and then said he was the Savior, why did they then kill him? Right now Nelson Mandela is being painted as a Saint (St. Mandela) and soon they are going to come to South Africa and hijack his image, and start worshipping him just like they did with Jesus. Paul of old once persecuted the disciples and apostles of Jesus and then turned around and cooperated with them after receiving a vision by the road to Damascus. Mandela received his vision in the Isle of Robben (Robben Island), instead of persecuting those who oppressed the Bantu, he quickly jumped in bed with the oppressors just to pacify us and keep us from not fighting back. It is no wonder then that most non-Bantu people in South Africa and/or Africa fear that when Mandela dies they will catch hell. They'll probably will. You can't plants seeds of misery and not reap havoc. You should know better.

I want freedom, fuck democracy!

Chapter Two

I don't like to kiss and tell, more especially to name-drop. Let those I've "smiled" with allow me to do it just this once.

Chulo and Lava are walking up Jorissen Street heading towards the Civic Theatre direction. They've just come from Pick 'n Pay with bags of groceries and now they are stopping by Debonair's to collect two boxes of pizzas. As they walk in, Chulo notices a medium height female with eyeglasses looking at him. He can't make out if the look is flirtatious or innocent. The woman is with a friend and at first it seems like it's a mother and a daughter, Lava noted. Chulo and Lava picks up the pizza boxes and head out and as they walk out, the woman looks at Chulo and goes giddy. They walk up by the robot, corner of Jorissen and Biccard Street. Chulo feels that the women are up to something; he looks back inside the shop from where he is and the medium-height woman waves at him and he waves back. From then Chulo knew that it was on. They wait patiently by the corner for the cats to crawl into the bag.

"Gentlemen," says Nobuhle. Nobuhle is the medium-height woman who is walking with S'phelele and they are carrying food parcels.
"How you doing," asks Chulo?
"It's a lovely day indeed," says Nobuhle.
S'phelele is not saying anything but smiling, whereas Nobuhle is taking the initiative. She is the kind of woman who goes for what she wants, they run you before you run them. The hunter becomes the hunted. Chulo didn't have to do much other than ask for

Nobuhle's numbers, the woman was already feeling him. In Braamfontein there is a lot of Nobuhle's just as there is a lot of Chulo's. They don't love but desire.

"Let me get your number so that I'll know it's you when you call me."

"Oh for sure!"

"What you guys up to?"

"Glad you asked that, we get together and we share your Steers with our Debonair's."

"It's for the kids."

"Where do you guys stay?"

"Alberton," says Nobuhle.

Lava is stone cold, not even reacting or interacting with S'phelele. Numbers were exchanged, comments passed and farewells said. Off they went Chulo and Lava still astounded by what has just transpired. They are ecstatic.

"Did you see that *mfana*? I told you that old women are stress-free when it comes to this game," says Chulo.

"*Uyaphusha lomfana?*" Lava comments as he smiles.

"Not me *mfana* but these black foxes of Braamfontein," says Chulo.

Later on that night Chulo got a text message from Nobuhle. The event took place in the afternoon and by night time a text read: "you are yummy just incase you didn't know. can't stop drooling ever since we parted."

"Yo son, look at this." Chulo shows Lava the sms.

"Mine is warm enough already to show her some action," Chulo boasts.

"Organize them and let's do the damn thing," Lava responds.

A week later, Lava, Chulo and the females met at Lava's place, nicknamed Shawshank. We, I was planning to sure-shag mine had she hadn't detected that that was my one and only intention - to stick her. Hey, stick-ment is the treatment of the day for these masses of broads. No one wants to settle down in a city like Jozi, *kwanyama kayipheli kuphela amazinyo endoda.* I don't know which meat they were talking about, whether it was gold or pussy - I don't know. But I would like to believe that it was the latter.

When the two females got in the house after work, we had planned that they were going to be laid on the couch, wined and dined, nicely and then stick-ment. For the better part of the plan, things progressed smoothly up until a point when I initiated sticking, my one jumped and claimed that I didn't love her and didn't care about her and that all I wanted was sex. Ain't no lie to that, sex had been on my mind from the day I laid eyes on that woman. Honestly, I never loved them.

"We barely know each other and now you talking sex, who do you think I am," questioned Nobuhle? From the moment I heard that sound coming from out her mouth, I just shut off and wished she was gone.

"Why do I have to be put on probation for something that you also enjoy?"

"We barely know each other and you expect me to just drop my panty for you just like that? Never!"

"But I thought we were feeling each other and besides, I've known you for over a week now so technically, this is not our first date. So therefore, we are very much acquainted."

"I still feel you right but listen to this, we hardly know one another and besides, you can't expect me to sleep with you in a place like this."

As a matter of fact, I wasn't gonna sleep with her but I was gonna have sex with her. Regardless of me having balls to drag her to the loo (toilet) to pursue sticking. What was I to do, Lava only had one bed that I could use but he was using it with S'phelele. The other bed was off-limits, it belonged to Jika and he didn't appreciate me using it as my love mat for all the females I would bring. He used to say that I'm reducing its mileage or some shit like that. That's why Nobuhle and me were posted up in the toilet / bathroom.

I had to let her go because she was getting on my nerves on her attempts of making me beg her. Lava didn't pursue sticking but was acting like a boyfriend and shit. Slow brothers! Timid men! We didn't even take them to the elevator, they saw their way home.

Chapter Three

Robbery is on the rise again by the Mandela Bridge. It's a nice architectural structure. It reminds me of the George Washington Bridge, Verrazano-Narrows Bridge and this other one I've seen in Central London going over River Thames next to the Ferris Wheel, park- it's a foot bridge. Amidst its sheer splendor, crime or robbery is well executed there because of its narrowness when it comes to the pedestrian walkway. You get cornered and there is never a chance or a passage to escape, the criminals just attach your property with ease. It could be that the bridge is ahead of its time, a time when crime is at the ultimate low, with all the White people living in the city. Gentrification for sure, is inevitable. I would like to own a piece too of the city space, just a pad.

Cellphones, wallets, jewellery, etc, are items that vulnerable pedestrians loose on an hourly basis on this bridge they named after Mandela, which connects Braamfontein with Newtown Precinct and the city centre of Johannesburg.

Walk up Jorissen from the Wits Theatre going towards Mzithos and Debonairs, take a right on Biccard Street and go down towards KFC (De Korte and Biccard) - you'll see an interesting change of scenery. By the time one gets to the KFC area, he is aware that he is now in West Africa no longer in Johannesburg, South Africa. Just go down on Biccard Street, pass Juta Street and all the way to Smit Street and turn left, head towards Simmonds Street, turn right and go up Simmonds. The African Brothers are muscling their way in for sure. What is stopping the South African Brothers to do the same, whether here in uMzansi or elsewhere in the world?

The other day I was checking out Youtube and Kwame Toure (Stockley Carmichael) was talking about voting and the so-called Black leaders that are portrayed as being the representatives of the masses. Voting is represented as being a once-off matter in every after 4 or 5 years. One's political participation is when he or she goes to the ballots whereas it should be an everyday thing. It made me think that this whole democracy issue is a joke just like BEE (Black Economic Empowerment) is a joke and such a blasphemous matter towards the poor and working class masses. There are things that are said but they are action-less. They say go vote, we will do such and such but that such and such never gets done and when you ask them what happened to such and such, you're viewed in such and such a way. Politics - a very funny (Mickey Mouse) business. Political parties are from the same mother who is a whore and forces her kids into political prostitution.

Chapter Four

I met this other very nice and lonely big mama the other day while walking with my homeboy. It was around Jorissen Street in the afternoon. She was looking down, told her to keep her head up. From that day on we kept in touch. I give her some fresh blood she gives me her froth pussy. Reminds me of Dingane of old, after the pussy Mzilikazi's mother. A way to a woman's heart is through her legs.

This one was so warm that the first time I ever pulled her close to me to get a hug, I almost ejaculated so I had to push her away from me. That was going to be so embarrassing because it was in broad daylight, and imagine having such a thing happening. That would have been something else. Some women will have you release the fluid way before you even enter their private organ. Some will fight you for so long that by the time you put it in there, you just cum. Then they feel cheated or shortchanged, that's their fucking business because they should not have made me beg for it or fight for it. The anxiety had gotten the best of me so I couldn't wait any longer.

Maybe when a man is going to see his ladyfriend he should release this dirty fluid first so that by the time he gets there he is ready for some action. The dirty fluid is embarrassing and such a self-esteem dropper especially when you know that this woman you're getting her for only just this once and you'll probably never see her again so you just want to give her something to think about.

I always get this though with big or well-fed women. Funny enough, the other day I bumped into this nice, tall and slender one that wiggled her tiny else as she walked. She must have been a couple of years older than me but I didn't care – I'm stupid!

I ran after her trying to pursue her name and number and she kept telling me that she was married. I looked for a wedding ring but I couldn't see any so I figured she was bluffing. When she told me that she was married I wanted to turn around and leave but couldn't because somehow I just wanted to stick around so I can finish ejaculating on my pants. Crazy stuff, hey? I didn't even touch her but the moment I go next to her and started talking with her, I just felt semen bubbling on my balls and rushing to come out on my penis. I just busted a nut on my pants with no vagina in sight, without manipulating my organ or whatsoever.

Maybe that woman uses *umuthi*. How can she make a grown man do that? Maybe I'm weak!

Anyway, back to my big one. I remember the first time I managed to convince her to come to Shawshank during her lunchtime so I can give her a sample. It felt like a milestone. I was scared and very unsure if she would be agreeable or not. I learnt that you'd never know until you try. It turned out that she was highly agreeable. I was shocked but at the same time excited. When you expect nothing and get everything - that is destiny.

I organized with Jika to give me venue so I can stick, and he agreed. When we were young or should I say when we were teenagers - all that we wished we had was venue for stick-ment purposes. For me, it started at age seventeen or eighteen. I had a late start when it came to dating and sex.

I can remember guys as far back as Standard Four (Grade 6), Standard Five (Grade 7), who were already into sex. Back then one would go to school with very old guys and women. Women would get pregnant or had kids already. Guys would be bunking (skipping) school because of illnesses such as sexually transmitted diseases and more. At Standard Six, my friend Mgavest had a "drop" twice in one year. Trying to fathom such back then would have been crazy. And besides, my mother and my granny would have given me a serious hiding (beating) with a *sjambok* for thinking such nonsense or associating with guys who were into that kind of lifestyle.

Jika gave me venue, he disappeared and I walked the Ma to Lava's bed. I closed the door and I started to think of how I was going to undress a senior lady like her.

"What time do you have to be at work," I asked?

"Anytime from now."

My palms started sweating, tongue was stiff, so I

froze.

I just froze.

I stayed frozen for a while.

A thought came, so I decided to start kissing and rubbing. She didn't protest. I read that reciprocity as a green light for me to proceed. I stood her up and took off her coat, shoes and while I attempted to unbutton and zip down her blue skirt, I was met with resistance. I didn't care because I knew it was just a last kick of a dying horse. Once the skirt was down, the blouse followed. I struggled to take off her panty hose and panty - a huge panty. I told you, this was a big mama I was working with. She had big love for a guy like me. Took off my Lee dungarees, my sneakers and was left with my Aeropostale underwear. I reached for a condom, took off my underwear and slipped the rubber on my organ. I'm doing all of this I'm thinking, she must not have a sudden change of heart and decide to get dressed and leave. Sometime these women can be disorderly like that. I spread the big thighs and I landed on her warm bosom. Wow! There is no need for me to stress the rest. All I can remember is her saying:

"Ifake yonke Chulo. *Ngiqedele toe!"*

Chapter Five

Braamfontein has changed. Braamfontein is changing on a daily basis. The other day, a new Eland monument was erected right where the ABSA Bridge used to be. CNA left, now you have Identity, Truworths and other shops. Clicks is still there too. Pick 'n Pay is making a killing without any competition whatsoever. Maybe there should be Woolworths to compete with Pick 'n Pay. Chicken Licken transformed to DeRego Chicken.

Long Bar is still happening, Veers is still the joint for Witsies. Now there is Spurs, luxury apartments in almost every corner of Braamfontein. There seems to be this obsession with the so-called Manhattan "style of living." That is messed up. Why can't they have a Braamfontein "style of living?" So now we must use New York City as our yardstick to determine how our residential places are arranged and designed? That is so fucked up. Maybe in New York City there is a so-called "Sandton style of living" or "Braamfontein" or "Cape Town" style of living. It's these town planners and developers who promote this nonsense. We must create our own.

What happened to that strip-club that once opened up on the building by Mandela Bridge, opposite the Audi dealership? It was hot and happening. Women there would strip to their natural skin. That joint used to get flooded by college and university students, horny bastards who went there to take photographs so they can go home and manipulate their organs. Or young women who now and again contemplated entering the trade of soliciting sex for bread.

Just the other day, Punk and me were driving around Yeoville looking for things to stick. And we bumped into this other nice one, light-skin one.

"*Unjani?*"

"I'm fine," her response was full of attitude, the attitude that suggested that I should go ahead.

"Look, where are you heading to," I asked?
I'm trying to sound confident and shit. This fine "foxy lady" was about to enter her building (flat) block when I called for her attention. I pulled to the side and jumped out of the car so I can get her digits.

"I live here, so I'm going in."

"Nice, nice! Can by any chance get your numbers so I can talk to you later on, seeing that you're in a rush?"

"Why not?" She said that with less resistance. I took her numbers down and promised that I'll be in touch. Punk and me we drove off and I took him to his place.

"Punk, you'll be a fool if you don't stick that thing tonight. Did you see how she was feeling you," asked Punk?

"I did Punk but I'm not sure if I can pull that stunt so soon. It's been barely ten minutes since I spoke with her."

"And so?"

"She might not be agreeable to come with me."

"All you have to do is to ask her."

"Okay Punk, I'll call her."

"Hello!"

"Hi!"

"It's me, I just met you now now, remember?"

"Yes I do! What's up?"

"Actually, what are you up to?"

"Nothing in particular. Why you ask?"

"Look, please come out! I'll buzz you when outside."

"Where are you?"

"I'm not far."

"Okay!"

"So," asked Punk?

"I'm going to fetch Punk."

"You see, what did I tell you?"

"No, you were right Punk."

"It's game my man, someone got to run it."

I dropped-off Punk and made a speedy turn back to the Foxy Lady's neighborhood. On the way, I called Lava to see if he was home or not, for venue. Guys with venue are vital if you're a game*boy*, every player needs his play station (venue). Lava was home and I knew that once the Foxy Lady agrees to get in the car and leave with me, I'll definitely stick her. I buzzed her from the outside and she came with her panties on her hand and I knew it was sticking that night. I tried to charm:

"You look hot!"

"Oh, thank you," she shyly responded.

After my comment or compliment and her response, there was silence. My mind was now tripping and I started concluding or assuming that she was in business, she'll probably charge me for sticking her. Anyway, I just didn't give a damn because if she was really in business of trading sexual favors for bread, she would have indicated.

I parked on Merle Street, outside Shawshank. I could see that my Foxy Lady's tongue was already bleeding from her licking of my double-edged sword, which I had coated with blood. I led her to the slaughterhouse, Shawshank. We entered

Shawshank, Lava and Jika was there and they were stunned to see such a beauty. We parked on the couch, made introductions and without hesitation; I invited her to my private room, the bathroom. I turned off the lights but her beauty illuminated the room. A beauty in the dark. Yes indeed, she was something else. Nice smooth body, smooth legs. Even thinking about her now, I get an erection.

I sticked, sticked sticked and sticked. My goodness, she was nice. The type that you just want to eat with your mouth. When I was undressing her blue jeans, she asked:
"Why are you doing this?"
"Because you're worth it," I said.

I'm not sure if that's exactly what I said or not but I knew that if I entertained talking she might outtalk me and talk me out of sticking her. Who wants to do such nonsense? She was on high heels, took off her baby blue jeans and landed her on the sink, her back behind the mirror and I could see myself as I made funny faces.
Stick-ment, is good for your health. The more the merrier. Always use protection so as not to catch HIV shit! ...but skin to skin (when you're circumcised) is always the best. You decide. Just remember to wash your dick after doing it.

A WOMAN FROM FICKSBURG (19-07-2009)

Thinking of her gives me an erection.
A woman from Ficksburg, what a beauty?
Smooth and fresh skin
Bathes on milk, her drying towel is cheese.
Pure and undefiled
I think I'm in love
I think she's in love
Quiet and yet her confidence is peaking.
A fly lady, stylish
Breasts like ripe tender figs on
A farm nestled under the berg
A woman from Ficksburg.

In my world she came like a dream
Inspiration to be precise.
The memory of how we met is etched on the canvas
of my mind.
Un poesis pictura, Sacred and Profane Love
A Titian, a Caravaggio, a beauty
A masterpiece without blemishes
Happy is the mother or father
Who birthed her.
But merrier is the man
Who will have her.
A woman from Ficksburg.

The brief moments we shared
Seems like a century of blissful
Pleasure.
But why did she choose to leave
The moment I met her?

She called last night crying her
Heart out about how much she
Misses me and love
I was at a loss for words
I told her I love her
"Till she comes back, I'll stay!
She's peaceful, suitable to be the one
Imagine traveling the world
With her.
Her carrying my tools on a Goyard
Making sure I look good.
She's a one of a kind
A pure and rare gem
A woman from Ficksburg
Sweet Seventeen!

Chapter Six

Funny enough, Mzitho's eatery (situated on the passageway in the building blocks that are surrounded by Biccard, De Korte, Melle and Jorissen) has been in business for as long as I can remember but there are hardly any renovations. People come and they come in numbers to fill their bellies. It's worse during lunchtime where one can see extremely long queues of hungry city dwellers lined up to purchase a plate.

Mzitho's prices keep rocketing every time. With all the money he's making, he can afford to buy out the next-door shops (buildings) and expand. People should be able to phone-in and order their favorite dish. I missed my plane to London in 2005 while I was busy entertaining my stomach grumblings with tantalizing "Pitoli" plate. Anyway, that's a story for another day.

It seems like Braamfontein is caught up in between being a student residential area and being a business district with lifestyle residential apartments. These are dynamics of urbanism (urban development and planning). It would be interesting for one to pursue a higher degree in Development Studies, focusing on urban renewal and regeneration.

Outside Civic Theatre, now known as the Johannesburg Theatre, there is a beautiful beautiful garden / park. A fenced park. A public park that closes its gates after and before working hours. What is the point of making the park public when the public has restricted access? Its greenery is good for the concrete jungle that Braamfontein is. The lawns are lusciously green with nice indigenous trees; it looks like a Highveld inside the city. The rural meets the urban – an oxymoron of some sort.

Liberty Life is on a mission to swallow all the small buildings neighboring it. There are bridges going every which way! Liberty Life is like a village of its own. Another oxymoron - a village in a city. It's good; it means they are in business, making money. They mustn't cry then and say recession is messing with them when their greed forces them to expand without control. It's like a woman who is loose but who refuses to use birth control. She falls pregnant from her thigh-opening activities and then she cries foul. Bullshit! You should have used a pill or loop or closed your legs, bitch!

There is this woman that I used to like her friend / roommate and this friend of hers had a cousin from Pretoria that I used to like too. I think they were all from Klerksdorp or something. They were like a crew and they used to always come and visit Lava and Jika at Shawshank. I first came to contact with them late 2006. Like I said, I liked her friend / roommate, Siphokazi. In retrospect, I think this Siphokazi only liked me when she was intoxicated. She felt loose and excited around me when she was under the pretext of alcohol.

Anyway, I didn't care; I just wanted to get with her - nothing more and nothing less. We would buy whiskey and invite them to Shawshank so we can get them frisky. Things never did go our way because once they boozed, they became rowdy and we had to kick them out without ever getting to stick them. Maybe the ratio dynamics never really balanced, there would be more of them than us or more of us than them. Or one of their boyfriend's would call and they would quickly jump out and leave. It was very frustrating because we all wanted to bone them, especially Siphokazi. Siphokazi was hot, tight ass, big boobs, body banging. Even interesting when she is drunk, she would start dancing with the other women and they would be doing freaky moves and shit.

Somehow someway, we never really got to stick them, or well for me- I never really got a chance to position myself nicely with her so I could tap her.

One time we organized some drinks from Tops in Melville and they were invited over. There must have been about four or five of them and there were three of us. The mood was nice and jolly. Siphokazi came with her hot hot hot chiskop cousin, forgot her name. I remember her so well; she was medium height, chocolate skin, simple and pretty. The moment she came we clicked. We blazed weed together that night, I remember. As it is in the bitch's nature, Siphokazi or Ngile - they deliberately disturbed my moment with Siphokazi's cousin. Fuck! I was pissed, seriously pissed but hey, what was I supposed to do? Exactly-nothing. I only managed to get her digits because I thought that maybe something might materialize.

Sometimes these females only like you only to compete with their friends or some nonsense like that. When her friend is feeling you they step in and confuse each other and thus throwing you off by their antics. They are very disorderly by nature. You find out that they don't even like you but they can pretend like they are interested only to just prove some oestrogen point. I just can never figure out these female species. I hate them and I love them. Honestly, I respect them more than the love-and-hate relationship I have developed towards them. I remember the first time I came to contact with this particular group of females. It was one night where Lava and Jika invited me to come through and go attend some music event at Baseline, Newtown Precinct. I can't remember who was performing and it is irrelevant. What is relevant is that midnight when the show was over, this group of females I didn't know then wanted to ride with us back to Braamfontein. We took them to Braam, Jika and Lava tried to run but I was nonchalant. We just dropped them off and we went our on way. I think Jika and lava loved those females but their game was lukewarm and they ran them on a very slow pace. I didn't care what was up then.

Another time when I came to contact with the females and I was told by the guys that it is the same females that we had given a ride to Braamfontein - Newtown the other night. It was when one of them, Siphokazi caught my attention. Mind you that these females were not particular or extra-ordinary than many other females but they had it going on. They were always coming through to Shawshank- to flirt with Lava and Jika, so I hear. When I came I said: "fuck the flirting and lets get into their drawers."

One night I came to see Jika and Lava and three of them females were there. No drinking but sobriety this time. They were checking out DVD's, somehow a cozy landscape existed.

Most guys I have mingled with say that most of the females they got to stick it was through association. Sticking by association is nice. When your dude is immunized and his thing brings a thing, chances of you sticking her friend are heightened. Look, you don't have to do any magic or wonders, just be nice and decent to her - you are more likely to stick. Maybe I should write a book on this phenomenon of sticking by association: STICKING BY

ASSOCIATION.

Chapter Seven

Rea Vaya, Rapid Bus Transport system is busy changing the landscape of certain areas of Johannesburg city. Some parts of town, robots are not working and traffic is hell. The road that goes around the Metropolitan Centre building by the Joburg Theatre- is chaotic, disorderly and irritating. The reason being that the BRT system needs the roads to be arranged in a certain order. Amos Masondo is re-arranging the face of the Johannesburg city centre. Roads in town too are a disaster; Commissioner Street from the Jeppe direction is out of control. Rissik, Market, Loveday and others - are being reformed to make way for the BRT system. Maybe when it is all said and done, Johannesburg will look and function nicely for a while before everything or the BRT system expires again, like many other systems.
Is Constitutional Hill / Court in Braamfontein or Hillbrow?

Jorissen Place opposite Braamfontein Centre is another beautiful building. Architecturally sound structure with its marble and granite facade.

GauRide, BRT, GauTrain, Metro Express and Business Express Rail are all programs or systems to help improve production and consumption of goods. Think about it for a second and agree. Matter of fact, you don't have to agree with it but do yourself a favor and think about it.

That temptress, Siphokazi and her squad? I had tried connecting with her so I can see her outside our boozing moments but never succeeded. I would call or text her to try and hook up with her around Braamfontein but she was always elusive, and I was getting impatient. As Punk would say: "she is acting like a super-bitch I can't handle."

I was busy with my things too so I ignored her completely. Why should I keep knocking my head against a stonewall? I can't do such nonsense, even if I'm pursuing sticking. Sometimes these women be thinking that they are the only ones with vaginas so they push the price up and shit. I wasn't bitter though she made me wait, I just had to find a substitute or substitutes to keep me busy while Siphokazi goes through her emotions.

One silly night, Ngile came with her squad but without Siphokazi. I was told that she was with her guyfriend. Anyway, we drank and blazed with the squad, as usual. They became chaotic - the usual, what's new? We kicked them out because they started screaming and drinking glasses were breaking. Nothing embarrassing than a woman who gets more drunk than you and starts acting foolish. That shit is embarrassing because now you have to baby-sit her. At that moment they became unruly and they started cursing and stuff.

Women and alcohol? A bad combination. Like R.R.R. Dhlomo once said in the 1940's in *Indlela Yababi*: "Alcohol is bad enough when men are abusing it, worse when women are." So women and strong drinks are a deadly mixture.

Like I said, we kicked them females out. Let me mention this, me and Ngile we never really got along very well. I don't know why but we just never did. She was cool with Jika and Lava but not me. Anyway, who cares? She was okay but had a skin problem on her face. She had dark marks / spots I think from chickenpox or something. Getting them outside the building after kicking them out of the flat (Shawshank) was also another mission. Once they were out of Shawshank they would make noise on the corridors as they made their way towards the elevators. The next-door apartment to Shawshank, an old couple lived there and they would always complain that we made noise and shit. What were they expecting? We were young guys in the city that hardly sleeps and they expect us to act church? No ways! The squad left and we went back to Shawshank to clean up the broken glasses and bottles and to drink some more.

Thirty minutes later after kicking out the females, Ngile came back crawling like a wet dog to apologize to the guys about their misbehaving. I really don't recall correctly what happened but I do remember picking up a fight with Ngile and we were pushing and cursing at each other and the next thing I saw I was on top of her sticking her. Don't ask me how it all happened!

Men, alcohol and women - a crazy mixture.

Chapter Eight

What is the difference between gangsta rap (rap) music and romantic-love music? The subject matter is different but the desired effect and influence is the same. Why do I say so? Let me tell you! Some say gangsta or rap music incites some individuals to be violent and aggressive. And some say love-romantic music incites others to be soft and to fantasize.

When it is all said and done- what about the freedom of choice, free agency? People are entitled to their freethinking and choice making. Such music can only excite you, influence you or incite you if you are any way, already harboring such intentions. Don't go blaming certain forms of media for individual's choice of weapons. These forms of media are their platforms to vent out their angers or frustrations, they are not teachers nor are they parenting platforms. Next thing they are going to be saying that this book I'm writing incite individuals to be promiscuous and shit. I'll tell them to go fuck themselves. Promiscuity has been going on for years, how can they blame this Braamfontein book?

That which starts sweet ends up bitter. That which starts sour ends up sweet. Yesterday and on Monday, Zwelinzima Vavi and his Union mobs went around vandalizing and trashing the city. Braamfontein was littered with trash on the streets. Could this mean that the country has gone to the dogs? Dogs tip trashcans in search of crumbs and leftovers, total scavengers. Fifteen years later, people's demands are still not being met. Before we even go striking - give us what we want. Give us exactly what we want, not just fodder to numb us and deceive our kids ever-empty stomachs. Don't give us what you think we want but give us this day our daily bread.

In a town like Braamfontein, news travel faster than the speed of an email or a text message. I say that to say this. One night, me, Jika and Lava we went party-hopping around town. This time we rode with Siphokazi and her crew. Siphokazi rode shotgun looking tempting as hell. We didn't speak much but I remember her demanding smokes, snacks and food. Students in a city like Braamfontein goes through hunger phases. The money they get from home or elsewhere gets depleted instantly. Cost of living is way too high in the city. That's why shit loads of females solicit the help of sugar daddies. But most of these guys, so-called sugar daddies treat these females from Braamfontein as appetizers and/or desserts. They have their main-squeeze at home; they just reach out to these Braamfontein females who are mostly students, for sexual favors. Most of these females don't realize that they get caught up on a trap where they trade sexual favors (sex) for bread, sex for airtime, sex for booze, sex for the payment of an Identity or Foschini account, sex for cheese. Who is to blame? As far as I am concerned, everyone is to blame, if not everyone, then no one is to blame.

When does one get time for all these women buzzing around Braamfontein? Maybe one should just take one bite at a time. Like Don Corleone, something in me says:
"A man's reach should exceed his grasp otherwise what is heaven for?"
Run game Runner!

I bought her some smokes and snacks with hopes that I'll be accorded sexual favors. Had to wet her beak. Some of these females have mastered the arts of the game. They'll milk as much as they can before giving it up. They'll just touch you, rub you, kiss you here and there a bit just to keep you hoping and wishing that sooner or later you were going to get it. Most likely you would have given up by the time she decides to open up legs or you would have forgotten about her and pursued another one from the bottomless pit.

We hopped and hopped up until it was time to call it a night. It must have been around 01:38 midnight and Siphokazi was still riding shotgun when we found a quiet spot and I tried rubbing her and kissing her, hoping that I'll stick. She didn't give. I tried to convince her to go to Shawshank but was ashamed to give me pussy at the company of Jika and Lava.

I was becoming impatient from all the pussy begging shit when I decided to circle a block while I think of what to do next. I was disturbed from my thoughts by a hand on my sex organ. The hand was like that one in the Adams Family flick. It tried to force its way down my Levi's jeans but was met with resistance from my Guess belt. I realized that if I act nonchalant, Siphokazi might abort her kind mission, so I quickly unbuckled my belt and lowered my jeans and underwear.

Oh, sweet joy I felt when her soft lips massaged my naturally ribbed roll-on. Thinking of that night gives me an erection.

She nibbled my organ as if she was in an intimate conversation with it. It's like she was talking to it or trying to convince it that next time it will get the real thing.

Who needs a real thing when one has been given

a heads up?

The organ sneezed some sweat a bit and that's when I knew that I was satisfied. I knew that I'd probably release some fluid once I was inside her. Fluid never comes out from a head. Oral or intercourse? Oral for me. That shit makes me feel like a King makes me feel good and relaxed. Funny enough, at times I didn't think any self-respecting men or women should be going down and sucking or licking another's genitals. That nonsense is nasty. Last time I went down on a woman was the day I stopped. She was one of those women I would get with when I was really really really bored – the last resort. One night the boys were running and I couldn't access the usual stuff so I called her.

"Where have you been," she asked?

"Been busy, you should know better," I lied.

"Stop lying coz I know you were not. You know what Chulo, I don't appreciate the way you've been treating me lately. Treating me like shit. You say you gonna come and you never do. What the fuck is up with that?"

That was a mouthful. Yeah! She can go on and on and on just running her mouth and giving me a headache. When me and her first began, we were tight but as I kept traveling up and down, we became less tight. Anyway, let me get back to the oral sex story.

After her running commentary of my conduct towards her, I told her that I was outside her house and that if she didn't come out I was going to leave. Like an unbelieving voyeur, she peeped out the window and said:

"How come you didn't say in the beginning? Gimme two minutes."

We went to Shawshank, and after a drink or two I tried to pursue sticking. She hit me on my hand. Do you know what this means? In Zulu you would say:
"*Wangishaya isandla.*"

Basically meaning that when you try to put your hand on her thighs, she hits your hand and you know very well that she is saying a big NO. But such act shouldn't dissuade you. The hand-hitting meaning I have just given is a shallow one. One can only get a deeper one when one is talking not when one is writing. Verbal expressions carries with them wholesome meaning, and vivacity. I just walked away pissed off and she went to the other room to listen to Kwaito and House music, and to drink some more.

Thirty or an hour later, she came crawling under the covers. I came conscious because I knew that the cat had decided to come crawling to the bag. I extended my hand and it landed on her breasts. I nibbled her nipple a bit before I went down south. Fondled her sex organ a bit and there was no resistance. I came alive and actively undressed her. I put on my government condom and I tried to enter her but she pushed me away and told me that she wasn't ready and that to make her ready I had to go down and kiss her vagina. Shit! I put one and two together and realized that if one doesn't go down I will not stick. Fuck it, I went down. The pussy smelled a bit so I closed my nose (held my breath) and started working. But fuck, you can't lick it and breath with your mouth at the same time. The nose has to function for breathing purposes. I went down again and got dirty. Yes, I got dirty. I started tasting some salty mucus like secretion. I wiped my mouth and that whole froth; mucus shit was even dripping on my moustache. Some sick shit. I stopped there and then, excused myself by saying that I needed to go pee.

Obviously, I was lying; I had to go scrub my face, tongue and mouth from her scum. When I came back I didn't even touch her, I was so nauseated. I just pled weak erection, and we slept. I have never been down there ever since, and that was five years ago.

Chapter Nine

I almost forgot the "*bhubesi*" incident. I wish Jika was the one telling this story because he would have told it with so much flair, vigor and concisely, compared to me. The reason is this, I was a participant and Jika was the observer. He who saw the event narrates it better than he who was a participant. Well, let me just try and do my bit of narrating the "*bhubesi*" story. The infamous "*bhubesi*" story.

I don't know what landed us in Kagiso. I'm lying, I do know - I have just remembered. We had gone there to see some females that we had called earlier on. When we got there they refused to go Shawshank with us. So we said: "Fuck them." We left, on our way we stopped by a petrol garage and bought some *kotas*. The stupidly fattening *kotas*. Nonsense *kotas*. *Kotas* that no self-loving human should be eating especially at that time of the night. The *kota* that township dwellers eat not knowing that they are slowly committing suicide. Digging their early grave. The *kota* after eating it you feel sick more than full.

Fucked up junk food. Worse than KFC and McDonald's junk.

Worse than junk sex.

Anyway, we bought *kotas* (township burgers), we ate them outside the petrol garage. They were nice indeed, no doubt.

We wiped our oily mouths, rubbed our fatty bellies and drove off. On our way while still in Kagiso, we stumbled upon two "loose balls" walking along the street sidewalk. *Yazi*, one-day *umuntu* will pick up *izipoki* thinking *osisi*? This city (urban) life we live has made us to find our women as commodities that we have to pursue for pleasure and relaxation. Has it always been like this or is this the way things have to be? A part of me says: "I don't know" and another part of me says: "I don't think so."

It was 21:49 on a Monday, where could they be going and what could they be up to?

"Slow down so we could find out what they are up to?"

We stopped right next to them and rapped.

"Ladies! How are you?"

"Fine!"

"Where are we going to?"

"Home."

"We going Jozi for some drinks, do you guys want to come?"

"Where in Jozi?"

"Braamfontein."

They looked at each other as if trying to convince themselves to go or not to go with us. Next thing we knew we were on our way to Shawshank with them. Talk about plastic morals! We are so fucked up for we find beauty in the hideous. Pursuing and satisfying our lustful desires. It is tough. It was a long journey from the West Rand to the Central Rand along the Main Reef Road. It was long in a sense that we had to keep them females excited about where they were going before they can even have a sudden change of heart. So music blasted the speakers as we made our way to the slaughterhouse.

We finally arrived in Shawshank and we confessed to them that there were no intoxicants to be imbibed. They were pissed and started acting up. We tried to comfort them but to no avail.

Time by now was around 23:30 or something like that. I knew that I wasn't gonna waste my time comforting mine when I should be humping her. I didn't play like that. I tried to convince her that if she is nice to me and her friend is nice to my friend - we will go look for a joint to buy booze. She resisted a bit but soon softened down. Took her to the balcony and started kissing and rubbing her, she pushed me away and said:

"You guys are unfair, you told us that we were coming here to drink but now you are doing this."

Crazy woman, who in her right mind is going to allow him or herself to be driven all the way to Jozi by strangers all in the pretext of going to booze in the fucking middle of the night? No one! But if any, then they might as well expect to get fucked in the process. I spoke with Jika that we should go to Veers and to other joints that sell liquor to get some drinks to loosen up our stiff broads. Lava was in dreamland in his room. We went to Veers and it was closed. We went to another *joyinti* and it was also closed. For crying out loud, who in the hell is going to stay open at to twelve on a Monday in the middle of a month? No one! Exactly. But to try and convince these broads was something else.

We went back to Shawshank and Jika went and searched for Lava's stash but there was nothing. Lava usually kept a stash of booze either under his bed or on the wardrobe. It's pass midnight and I'm getting restless and irritated. I went to my one. She was seated on the couch; I grabbed her by the arm and led her to my favorite room. I started rubbing her, fondling her, undressing her, kissing her and convincing her that I was prepared to be her boyfriend. She kept pushing me away up until her pants and panty was by her ankles. I fucked the crap out of her and left.

Jika called me the following day telling me that I acted like a lion (bhubesi). I fucked her like a lion. I pursued her like a lion. I fucked her and left her like a lion leaving its kill only after tasting it. What the fuck did she expect? I was a hungry lion for sure. I had to steal that pussy in the middle of the night like a thief. Jika tells me that she kept calling me "ibhubesi". I don't know whether it was a compliment or what. But either acting like a lion or being likened to one is a compliment by itself. I sticked her faster than a rabbit gets fucked. True indeed, I gave her a good stick-ment. Jika never forgets that "bhubesi" incident.

Still on the issue of sex, Tony Parsons wrote on junk sex on an article for GQ magazine titled "An Overdose of Junk". Tony Parsons offers very interesting perspectives that are symptoms commonly found in big cities (urban space) of South Africa and in the world. His first two opening lines are as powerful as forces of evil. He says:

"Ah, but it is a degraded, despoiled age we are living in, where everything seems a corrupt imitation of what it used to be, an age where the letter has been replaced by junk mail, the traditional Sunday roast with potatoes and gravy has made way for junk food and the blissful, restorative eight-hour kip has become junk sleep, where you toss and turn and rise from your bed exhausted. Junk nation. Junk planet. Junk age. The worst of the lot is junk sex - sex when you honestly wished you had saved that erection for later, sex when you pumped it up when you didn't really need it, sex that you remember with the same indifference as last night's takeaway curry."

But how did things come to this, and why? Is it safe to put blame on globalization? Oh fuck, what am I doing? I don't want this narrative to be another academic issue with ideas and thought-processes that are well debated, argued and advocated. Tony Parsons said it well so why should I take or add from what he said? What would be the point? Junk sex is as junk as junk food; it is as junk as that "township burger" we gobbled in Kagiso before I was even referred to as a hungry lion.

Chapter Ten

Braamfontein sits above the Johannesburg (Randjeslaagte) City Centre; Parktown, Berea, Hillbrow, Doornfontein, Johannesburg, Newtown and Vrededorp surround Braamfontein. Remember the Wanderes Stadium, Krugers Park, Joubert Park, Burghersdorp, Ferreira's Town, Coolie Location, Marshalls Town, Malay Camp, Government Square, Marshall Square, Market Square, Von Brandis Square, Union Ground, Native Location, Prospect Park, Brickfields, Frenchfontein and Kaffir Location?

Braamfontein dates as far back as 1853 when it was a farm before the gold rush of 1886. South Africa's premier educational institution, the University of the Witwatersrand is situated in Braamfontein.

Imagine if God were or was to charge us for our thoughts. You want to think of something, you pay first. Just imagine that, for every thought that one thinks, money is spent. For negative thoughts, God charges double. Just think about that, it will be ridiculous. People will stop thinking and doing negative things. Maybe only the rich will or would afford to think negative thoughts. Oh no, that will be dangerous, the rich will always be doing more harm on the poor just because they can't afford to think such thoughts. Maybe God can or might say, we can think any thoughts we want, the rich and the poor but He will only charge us when we decide to entertain them then He will charge us. Will that mean that our dreams, wishes and thoughts will have an expiry date?

Your thoughts are only available to you for a limited time only. That would be really fucked up. I think the day when God chooses to do such He will seize being God. When our ancestors charge us for pleading our cause of righteousness with or to God and the gods. I don't think that is how things are naturally organized because such behavior will destruct the order of things. One will not be in control of his or her destiny. One will be in the process of pursuing something next thing a notifying message bleeps up and say:

"Please recharge, your limit will be reached soon."

The so-called Satan or Son of Perdition will be stealing vouchers from God's angels and selling them at a discounted fee or maybe since the negative thoughts are from him, Satan would probably leak them to his followers for free but on condition that one forsakes positive thoughts and pursue the hideous. I can see one of Satan's verses saying: "Blessed is he who has more and giveth not to his brethren for he shall be given more." Followers of that Fallen Angel they call Satan would probably sell negativity to their fellow brethren on the planet earth. That would be the day when churches go out of business because no men will depend on a preacher that has limited access to God's inspiration just like them. There would be a new form of greed. I don't know what type of greed that would be but damn sure - a different and a funny greed.

Imagine reading a Bible and get no meaning or ideas, matter of fact, you don't even want to get them ideas because you know that money you will loose if you entertain such thoughts or inspiration. That will definitely put preachers out of business and dry their storehouses because there will be no more tithes, offerings and donations. Imagine what it would do to the whole issue of blessings if God were to charge us a price for every blessing we have and will have. We would stop imagining first of all, secondly, we won't even be able to communicate with Him and our ancestors, because we will definitely run out of our vouchers while still busy trying to formulate our prayers and anticipating the kind of blessings we might receive. We will never be motivated to do anything.

There would definitely be a spiritual, moral, mental and physical recession in a depression.

Chapter Eleven

Lunchtime some time last year, I was walking with Punk on Jorissen Street right by the Wits theatre. We bumped into this very nice working one. She was on her way to a jewelry shop. The lady was fine, fine is an understatement. She qualifies for an overstatement of beautiful. Anyway, what is the difference between a lady that is fine or pretty or hot or sexy or beautiful or all that or wow or amazing or stunning, etc? Beauty is in the eye of the beholder. So this one particular lady was fine, very fine. It was love at first sight. Let me slow down, it was not love at first sight, it was lust at first sight. I wanted to walk her to where she was going but I thought it was better to just grab her digits and call her later. We parted ways - she had to go make use of her thirty minutes lunchtime and me and Punk had to go see his friend somewhere on De Korte Street and then to Pick 'n Pay for pap and stew or *Ouma* bread? I'm not sure.

We attended Punk's matters and after them we walked to Pick 'n Pay. Pick 'n Pay is buzzing around lunchtime. Can you believe that Pick 'n Pay is the only grocery store in the whole of Braamfontein that caters for the needs of its city dwellers, tie wearers and book pushers (students)? It's ridiculous, hhe! Well, please believe it. The owners of that Pick 'n Pay shop must be raking in millions every other week.

They are making a killing. Monopoly at its best. If I was a drug dealer, I would post up in front of Pick 'n Pay, it would be my corner bodega. I see a clan of garbage hungries, poor and the destitute, also plying their trade in front of Pick 'n Pay. The store has resurrected the neighboring shops; taxis to Yeoville and else where are even picking up people from outside these shops. Please, let's have diversity, competition and choice so we can see where the value of our hard earned rand is going. I love competition; I'm highly competitive on anything I find interest in. I forgot her name but I know she was from some township situated right inside Krugersdorp. Funny enough, the lady took a serious liking at me instantly. I texted her my numbers and she called me back asking when will I see her, you know - spend some time with her. A date or something like to it. Hunters like me, they become uneasy when the prey turns around and hunts the hunter. Imagine a lion being pursued by a Zebra? That shit ain't happening. It is not on.

That's disturbing the order of things. I still think like a "traditionalist" but act like a "modernist" when it comes to matters of the heart, women and sex.

For the next following days or weeks, we kept missing each other. When she was busy I wasn't and when I was busy she wasn't. We kept in touch on the phone. She would call me and I would text her. All along I was trying to save some money so I can go for drinks (water, tea or coffee) with her during her lunchtime. I couldn't arrange to see her after work because when she knocks-off at 16:00, her lift club would be waiting for her outside her work. So I kept trying and working on catching her during her lunch breaks. I remember, I had saved enough money to take her out for dinner to my favorite restaurant, Sushi by Zoo Lake, Parktown. I ended up spending the money on something worth my while because she was fuckin taking forever to come around.

Chapter Twelve

What is this non-sense I have been hearing on the news? Bheki Cele, Fikile Mbalula and Nathi Mthethwa are talking cowboy talk. They are talking about amending the law and Constitution to make way for a trigger-happy police force and a society. One is not going to be able to tell the difference between the cops and the robbers. Like my man Mos said, nowadays you can't tell between the cops and the robbers, they're all partners with no conscience. Gun-toting partners. These people have been watching too much cowboy movies. Wait and see, no one is going to kick doors in the White communities; no police is going to shoot-to-kill White or Indian and Coloured criminals but Blacks. Black men, you are under attack. Where is Batman when Two-Face is pointing his itchy finger trigger at us. Why can't Agliotti rat-out his partners in crime and the trigger-happy police go and arrest them or "shoot to kill" them?

They are criminals.
Band of robbers.
Gadianton robbers.
Witches.
Blood suckers.
Band of thieves.

An eye for an eye makes the world blind! Our leaders have lost the plot. A White farmer kills a Black man in North West mistaking him for a guinea fowl (dog or baboon). Aren't they not criminals? Terrorizing our Black sisters and brothers, mothers and fathers. What the fuck is up with that? This shit is nasty, makes me want to throw up.

Desmond Tutu, Nelson Mandela, FW de Klerk - talk some sense to these new guys. Both of you share a medal for PEACE, remember the Nobel they gave you?

Criminals are going to band together and they are going to overthrow the government, you wait and see. Silly me, there is no difference between criminals and cops. Government is the biggest criminal, a mob, and a gangster who sits in parliament and discusses how he is going to screw up you and me in a smooth way. One of us speaks out, they are quick to silence you, kill you or imprison you. Evil will never reign over good forever. A time is soon at hand for goodness to prevail over evilness.

We voted for these men to lead us in to righteous paths and yet they are still suspicious of us.

War, War, War!!!

Why they never shot and killed Johan Nel when he went around spreading death and mayhem on Black people in Swaartruggens?

Wasn't that a criminal activity? Where were the police? This is all bullshit. Let's prepare for WAR!

Teach us how to pay our bills. Teach us we must solve our problems. Teach us how we should stand on our own and not depend on your grant (welfare). Teach us how to respect our elders so that our days may be long on this planet earth.

Teach us nation building skills, not riffraff and garbage of this world. You feel me!

Who in the fuck is advising our mad Police Commissioner? I hope it's not the former New York City Mayor. The FBI? The CIA?

The IRA? Who? Don't they know that you kill and be killed?

Young Black men, they are going to murder us all.

Be careful and watch your back, always. Don't forget to stay strapped, and stay awake!

Tupac said:

"You want to last be the first to blast."

And yeah, fuck the police and fuck the criminals. That's right, I said it. Allow me to say it again: Fuck the police and fuck the criminals.

I can hear someone saying: "He's an angry Black male."

Isn't the White men being an "angry White men" when he wants justice (revenge) for what Osama bin Laden "allegedly" did in 2001, September 11? Why can't he turn the other cheek and sing a hymn that says: "Forgive Osama for he knew not what he was doing?"

Why do I always have to be the understanding one?

Tutu and Mandela must tell them to go and reconcile with Afghanistan, be on some "truth and reconciliation" nonsense like you did to us.

Why am I then a bitter or "angry Black male" for wanting justice from all the hell I have been catching? Someone is a hypocrite and yet he claims to be a "Christian"!

I remember when I used to foolishly go to church they used to talk about this "phenomenon" called REPENTANCE! I hated to hear that word because it didn't make sense to me to go to another man and tell him what I've been doing "wrong" as if God didn't see me do it. That Bantu knowledge used to say: you're not supposed to be perfect, you're supposed to stay balanced.

Anyway, they used to say that repentance was or

is a painful process that leads to forgiveness and everlasting peace. They said you must acknowledge the wrong you've done and then feel SORRY for it, CONFESS to your church leader(s) who are the eye for God, ABANDON the wrong or wrongs you've been doing, RESTORE everything that has been damaged by your wrongdoing, and then you can go living a blessed life.

SCAR = SORRY+CONFESS +ABANDON+RESTORE

No one has ever approached me and said sorry and gave me back what he took from my forefathers.

Talk about hypocrisy! Maybe that's why I left their church and decided to follow God who wants what is right by me and for me.

Talk about a scar, we got a lot of scars.

Lot of delinquencies we are suffering from as Black people will seize as soon as we draw closer to our God. We've been praying to the wrong God for so long no wonder why our prayers are not being answered, we sink more and more into the abyss.

America and other Western countries are wise for they know very well that you can't kill and not be killed. You can't touch their own kind and not expect retribution (justice) but when they touch our kind we must reconcile? That's an injustice. Anyway, we never going to win while we play their game, their way and in their playing field. We are always going to be following their rules. Follow follow follow- for how long? We are very intelligent, way intelligent than the White men, and he knows this and that what keeps him awake and scheming on how to constantly keep us asleep.

The devil can kill you and can kill me, it don't matter- others after us will come and avenge for us otherwise God of the Bantu people will seize being our God. When I talk about our God I'm not talking about the one that has Jesus, I am talking about the one that is neither a He nor a She, the Most Ultimate, the one that Has Been and Will Always Be. I'm talking about the One we should be praying to. The One that hears our prayers. The One that will never let us down. The One that gets offended when we run around praying to foreign gods, Jesus and their God. The God of our forefathers will never forsake us! Ask those that know the way to draw closer to the God of your forefathers. Seek and you shall receive. Don't stay in the wilderness (darkness) like the Israelites of old when Moses was trying to get them to the Promised Land.

Fear no man but God!

I wonder what these people are going to tell their God when we get to where we are going after inflicting so much pain on us. Maybe they don't believe in God, maybe they worship the other God.

Stop hurting us, please! If you don't listen now, when will you ever listen? Whites and Blacks oppress us and they need to stop. Just let us be, please. Stop bullying us. We are not as "wise" as you so don't rub our "foolishness" in our faces. Don't say you were never warned! Our God didn't make us to be your toys so you can toy with us as you please. Let us be! We want to be left alone so we can reconcile with our God on our own without your interference.

You keep spilling blood of these little ones, why? Do you feed on our blood? If you do, then I'll say you're a vampire.

You need to be exorcized!

Remember what Wycleff Jean said in that Amadou Diallo track? He said that he could hear the spirit of Diallo calling for justice. He even went as far as saying that "ten thousand chariots with no riders are on their way to America, I hear the tribe singing."

Chariots with no riders are on their way!

Crazy stuff, hey?

But you probably don't care but that's fine because the tribe will catch you when you least expect it. Does a housekeeper or house owner know when the thief is coming to rob his house? No! The thief comes the night you least expect it. Just as the sharks still follow the path where the African slaves (our relatives) used to travel on the slave ships, the same sharks will show the tribe the way to the Americas, the "chariots with no riders" will join with the spirits of the custodians of this land and will overthrow the descendents of those that dealt them that heavy blow.

Didn't you know that?

Once that is done, we will stay here for a season and some will be allowed to return home and others will choose to remain and live in harmony with the custodians of this land, for a season.

So no matter what you do to us, our God will never let us down! Amen to that!

Okay, back to my game running expedition about my Krugersdorp game. One day, she agreed to meet me for lunch but I was broke. I didn't tell her I was broke but I didn't take her to a place where I knew I would be challenged, financially. So I just went with her to a Tea Room somewhere around Braamfontein. Matter of fact, it was a bar. Managed to get her a can of Coca Cola and I boosted my energy with a bottle of Black Label. It was a hot day and the beer sizzled the heat off my fuming body. It was nice. We chatted about this and that through out her lunchtime. I was feeling her and she kept asking me when am I going to come visit her in Krugersdorp.

"Don't worry, we will arrange something," is what I kept telling her. Crap, what was I supposed to say? All the time there on our bar rendezvous, her boobs and thighs were giving my dick a headache. I seriously needed a strong dose of Panado.

The woman was hot, pretty and whatever you want to call a woman that looks like her. I was feeling this woman. I wanted to get with her so bad. I wanted to fuck her. She looked like she had a kid or two. I asked her but she denied it. I didn't care. I just wanted to stick dick, not to raise another man's kid - I was NOT interested in that shit. Get your own and raise your own. Time flies when you are having fun. She had to go back to work. I hugged her, gave her a kiss on a cheek and I stayed behind to squeeze the last ounces of what was left of my beer bottle. I ended up ordering two more. I stumbled outside the bar with an interesting step.

NO ONE HAS THE RIGHT TO KILL ANOTHER BUT EVERYONE HAS A RIGHT TO PRESERVE HIS OR HER GOD GIVEN LIFE, BY ANY MEANS NECESSARY!

LET'S TRY AND RESPECT EACH OTHER'S SPACE! WE DON'T HAVE TO LOVE EACH OTHER BUT LET'S RESPECT EACH OTHER!

<u>Respect</u> is greater than <u>love</u>!

BUT BEFORE ALL OF THAT IS SAID, JUSTICE MUST BE DONE OTHERWISE OUR PEOPLE WILL NEVER KNOW PEACE UP UNTIL THEY'VE MADE PEACE WITH THE ANCESTORS, GODS AND GOD. THE SPIRITS OF OUR DEPARTED WILL ROAM THE EARTH AND TORMENT OUR SPIRITS UP UNTIL JUSTICE IS DONE TO PACIFY THEIR SPIRITS SO THAT THEY CAN THEN RE-UNITE WITH THE SPIRIT OF THEIR LOVED-ONES IN THE WORLD OF THE SPIRITS.

Chapter Thirteen

The winter is almost over and the females can't wait to shed off their winter coats. One can see these young college women making sure that every time there is a sunny day - long jeans are traded with short pants and T-shirts. Who likes winter? I love summer more than I love winter. Winter is a season where one packs some fat in the body and tries to burn it off in spring in preparation for summer. Funny enough, you will start storing fat from autumn till the end of winter and hope that you will shed it all off in just three months (spring), never. Three months is not enough for shedding off all those kilos. Some people struggle to off-load. Loading is far easier than off-loading. Some you see even during the summer trying to burn only to load again in autumn. It is some funny shit. I think the best way is to maintain. Consistency baby, consistency - nothing much to it. I agree, for one to loose he doesn't have to do anything but to win it's hard because one has to do something (put in some work). So it becometh for each man to choose whether to do something or to do nothing.

Ngile kept away from Shawshank for quiet a long time. She knew that I wanted Siphokazi as well as her cousin from Pretoria. Siphokazi was hot, big boobs, thick ass and light skin and always chiskop. Her cousin was always chiskop too, plus they both smoked weed. I remember the time when they came through Shawshank and we just blazed the rest of the night away. These women were hot; I was feeling them both at the same time. Matter of fact, they were confusing me because I had feelings for both of them and I didn't want to choose just one of them. They were sexy, good for sex. Have you heard people say: "Wow, that's a sexy car? Oh, wow, that's some sexy apartment?" As if you are going to have an intercourse with a car or clothes or something that they consider to be sexy. No wonder why everything has been reduced to just SEX. It is all junk and sex has become a meaningless thing with no substance, value or pride. It is like eating food but still feeling hungry. It is time we go on a sex diet, sex fasting or something. But before we go there, let me finish up narrating some of my sticking escapades.

You know, I am reminded of this one I went home with one morning from a club thinking I was going to stick, and she told me that she was bisexual. If she were bisexual how come she wouldn't let me stick her? Should I tell you the story or not? Let me think about it.

One time, we had another one of our sick parties. Women came through and we invited some of our own women that were outside the Ngile group so we could enhance our chances of sticking, big time. They came, we drank and we smoked and it was fun. I ignored Ngile's group because they started acting like "super-bitches that we can't handle." Unfortunately, the group we had invited had to go early thus leaving behind Ngile's crew. You know that these females from Braamfontein that are students, don't mind paying you a visit every other day especially when they know that you always feed them with either food or booze. Makes me wonder why guys don't attempt sticking such needy females. They are in abundance and ready for the killing for crocodiles like us like the wildebeest in the Serengeti during the great migration. When Ngile's group noticed that they were the only group left behind, they started acting disorderly -

what's new about that? Remember that Siphokazi was not around. She chose not to show up because she was aware that I was aware and that her crew and my crew were aware that I was two-timing them plus I wanted to three-time Siphokazi's cousin from Pretoria.

What a beast I was? Fuck it, somebody got to do it. I was just playing my part. They were disorderly, we called them to order and they decided to bail, so they left. Me, Jika and Lava plus two other guys- we continued with our drinking and socializing.
The other two guys left two hours later. Thirty minutes after they had left, there was a buzz on the door, and it was none other than Ngile. All her crew had been taken away (fetched) by their "boyfriends" but except her. I think she didn't have a boyfriend. She was a nice woman but her face had a lot of chickenpox marks that had disfigured how she looks, tremendously.
The security guard on the ground floor would always blame me for making Lava and Jika to be disorderly when it came to abiding to the flat rules of not making noise past a certain hour. We didn't care, I didn't care - why do we have to seek permission from someone if we want to enjoy our drinks, smoke and sex when we feel like? Ngile was a bit sober now and she wasn't drinking. We were by Lava's room listening to some music and shit. She joined us and we just chilled. We started picking on her and she started picking on me. I wasn't interested in fighting with her but sticking her. Hey, once beaten twice shy. So I said to myself, once your thing always your thing - what's there to conquer? What is there for her to resist anymore? So we just hung out in Lava's room and we was just listening to music and sipping our

cocktails, Seagram's Gin and Coke.

Ngile and me were fighting right, verbal argument. Tension equals to attraction, right? She scratched me on my arm for no apparent reason. I was pissed. I wanted to punch her right in her mouth for doing such shit but I restrained myself, which is hard to do when you are intoxicated. I am not new to alcohol. I believe you can still use what good is left of your brain to reason. Fuck, I am lying, alcohol alters your thinking. Anyway, I was raised better than that, so I didn't dead her on the mouth. I told Jika to discipline her but they just laughed at me like I was a comedian (a joker as my friends in Lagos would say). I went and grabbed Ngile by her arm and I started reprimanding her and shit but she was just looking at me like I was a fool or something. I grabbed her by her dark navy jeans and I undressed her, I vividly remember even the panty (small number) she was wearing. What a freaky bitch! She asked me what I was doing and I told her that I was teaching her a lesson for being disorderly. I laid her on the bed and took off her jeans and panty. I don't know where Jika and Lava were and I didn't care. I grabbed my rubber and got strapped. She just laid there on the bed with her hands on her eyes. I touched her pussy and it was wet and shit. I opened her legs and I entered her. Thinking of that night is giving me an erection already. Wow, the pussy was juicy wet and warm. Slip 'n slide. I sticked her like crazy - from the bedroom bed to the bathroom sink (so I could see myself on the mirror) and back to the bedroom wall so I could nail her. The pussy was nice and I stole it like a thief.

Back on the bed, she got on top of me and she started showing me a trick or two. My dick just stood there solid as a rock, and stared at her. She sticked me nice too, I ain't gonna lie about that. Our body language was fucked up because when she wanted me to do her she had to put up a fight and provoke me.

I miss that bitch and the unique way we used to communicate. Is it true that once your woman always your woman? How really really true is this? You ago out with a woman and you stick her nice nice, things happen and you part ways. You have already conquered her, taken her pride away. So even when she sees you and you want to stick, she might put resistance at first but to no avail because you have already fucked her, what is there to prove or conquer? You can stick ten things and treat them nice - break up with them; they'll always have a soft spot for you. Funny enough or sad enough, even when they are married, they are always in covert thoughts and entertaining pastime thrills of that guy they used to mess with or never got a chance to mess with. Women are funny species men can never understand because they themselves don't understand each other or one another.

I think young people should be discouraged to premarital sex so that such can be prevented when woman is married but still harbors soft spots for her ex-boyfriend(s) and shit. That is nonsense. But then again, who am I to advocate such when I am a victim and a victimizer. I am part of the problem that I want to be part of the solution of.

Maybe men should start growing their penises back like lizards do to their tails and start being man about everything. I also think that a woman who harbors such inclinations should be let loose, how long is she gonna have to live like that? She must go to where her heart takes her - leave the man's ancestor's kids behind and also give back *izinkomo zamalobolo*, and then she can beat it like Michael Jackson. Like I said, the twenty-first man must be a man about everything. This feminine (metro sexual) behavior amongst us men is fucking us up and fucking up things. Women think they are men because they earn more than men. Men think they are women because they are too much understanding and agreeable to every other silly nonsense that women want or talk about. What happened to the African men, have they gone underground or they are busy strategizing? Whatever it is that they (we) are going, let us do it quick before it is too late. People like me never despair, we are optimistic. As men, let us go back and ask our forefathers (fathers and grandfathers, and uncles) how they did things back then and what can they teach us in these trying times and dying days we live in. We must do away with these modern men types and magazine carbon copies of what writers and editors fantasize about and pass it to us as if it is papal bill. It is time we start respecting ourselves but if we can't respect self at least let us respect the heritage. Maybe then, only then- we can change the world for the better one-day at a time. Whose responsibility is it to make the world better and habitable for the next generation? Me! You! I can't be taking pride in or on how many women I have stuck. Compare me to a guy who has never stuck a thing - what is the difference between him and me? He is innocent and I am not. Innocence is bliss.

Nowadays shit like AIDS is not playing, it is really fucking up men and women and if I am and / or if we are not careful it is going to wipe us out all just like the floods did in the days of Noah. Polygamy is the only way out to prevent such. When they say that destruction won't be by water this time but fire - AIDS is the burning fire that is going to burn us all like an angel of death. Head up, eyes open and condomise if you can't live the high law of polygamy, and if you can't abstain, otherwise you are going to feel the fire.

The truth is, whether I love these women or not, what is expected of me is to make babies and raise them right. We can't reduce everything to money. I hear people say to have kids in these days is costly. Bullshit. If you have land, you, your women and your kids can work it to yield fruits, raise cows, goats, chickens and stuff. Get out of the city, an African does not know or respect the concept of the city.
The city cripples an African's way of life (lifestyle). For example, how do you slaughter a goat or cow in your complex (townhouse) with bylaws on your ass and lack of space? As an African, you have to feed your ancestors at least once a year just like those Europeans do to their gods, the likes of Jesus. You can't even burn the holy incense, *impepho* to pray, with fire (smoke) detectors around. We are ashamed of burning *impepho* because we think it is embarrassing yet the Indians, Catholics and others- burn incense. Straight to the depths of hell if we forsake our gods and our customs. It is time we pray to our God and gods and not foreign ones- no wonder they never hear us when we have been exhorting them for years. We are in these flats, townhouses, condos and stuff and our ancestors don't even know where we are because we haven't invited them to where we are to protect us and our (their) kids. Think about that! Do something about that!

Chapter Fourteen

Let me tell the story of this one named Gabaza. She was okay, she was not spectacular- you know, an average woman she was. I would always see her around and all of a sudden, I developed a liking on her. She was a brown-skin lady and not too short. She hailed from Hazeyview. Mpumalanga just above Mbombela. She was busy pursuing her undergraduate degree in Linguistics. Every time I see her I would always joke about this and that with her and she used to giggle and stuff. I was not sure whether she liked me or not or just that she enjoyed seeing me "tickle" her or what. What I did know is that I wanted her, I wanted to do her badly. She adorned a nice petite ass that would peep out and show nicely when she was wearing a viscose skirt. She had the country (farm) elements about her. Us city dwellers love such women, we prey on them. We are what R.R.R. Dhlomo used to refer to back in the thirties: *omashaya bakhothe*. Ask a "proper" Zulu speaker to explain such to you. Anyway, I told myself that one-day, I would nail her.

That day didn't take long to come. What? Three months? That is not too long for a scavenger like me. I can wait a year, five years or even ten for as long as the carcass is still edible. I invited myself over to her place one afternoon, she told me that she was home and that it was fine I could come through especially since she wasn't doing much except cooking. She lived in a flat (compony) right next to where now the Eland Monument stands. These are or were student residences, an evolution of student residences way before there was even South Point and them - which is a modernized compony. These were one-bedroom apartments that were now converted through partition to house about six or eight students on a one-bedroom apartment. You can't even breath in such places let alone think. A shameful place, an urban Mshenguville. Talk about a squatter house, you talk about such living arrangements meant for the unknowing and desperate and strapped for cash students. Imagine White students living in such squalor. Miserable places! Can you imagine it? If you can't, don't worry because you are not the only one who can't imagine such. Besides, these unknowing Blacks who are from outside Gauteng and some from inside Gauteng- love the fact that they are living in a flat in town. Just like the other day on Jorissen Street, this nice female who looked like a first year student, stopped my friend and me and asked us how to get to Berea. She had to go there and look for a flat. She said that she was from Daveyton on the East Rand (Ekurhuleni) and yet she didn't know that Daveyton or Thokoza or Tembisa was better than Berea. We told her not to go and stay there. Berea had become a slum, a Kaffir Location just like Alexandria is. Such places should be demolished- they have expired. People deserve better. These places like Alex or Tembisa breeds' diseases that are seen and not seen. They should move people to clean and decent housing environment, knock down the walls of these Kaffir Locations, pour paraffin or C4 and watch them burn.

Landlordism is such a bitch. When the land is exhausted, one must move elsewhere.

Living in a flat is such an interesting experience for them.

Even if the elevators don't work, they still marvel to the fact they can boast to their friends at home that they are living in a flat, not Soweto or Alex. But anyway, that is not the issue at hand right now, the issue at hand or in question is my Hazyview one, Gabaza. Punk tells me that he even attempted running or sticking, I don't know. Punk's accounts are always questionable since his narratives always leave you in doubt of whether they did happen or didn't happen. Anyway, that is just Punk, lying even when there is no need to. He is older than 21 years but he still buckles down to peer pressure and he lies to try and appear on the good light amongst those that are actively sticking. You don't have to claim you have it when you know very well that you don't have it. There is always a time to admit when you haven't won. I signed myself by the security guard, gave him my proof of identification and ascended on the stairways to the seventh floor, elevators didn't work and they haven't worked since Braamfontein started becoming desolate. I knocked on the door and she opened for me and quickly whisked me to her bedroom, which was smaller than solitary confinement. There was only a single bed and a small study desk. She instructed one of her roommates whom she was going to share her meal with to continue or finish up the cooking while she plays the host.

She had a floral dress that one can mistake for a night (sleeping) dress. It was one of those with front buttons from the chest to its hem that was slightly above the knees. The moment I sat on the bed I knew that my time was ticking and I had to act. I moved right next to her and I started whispering sweet-nothings but to no avail. I kept pushing anyway. Somehow someway, I managed to get her on a kissing mode and she was very reciprocal. By this time my pants (jeans) and shoes were already decorating the floor. I placed her on my lap and started caressing her firm shooting breasts.

Her skin was nice and smooth with no blemishes.

Tried unbuttoning her dress but I was met with resistance. I placed her on top of me while I was in a seated position. We kissed on this position for a while up until she told me that it was enough. I relaxed a bit and my dick was solid as a rock and it kept on pounding and shit. She stood up and started heading for the door, I quickly grabbed her by the hand to stop her from leaving me in such a mess. She told me she was going to the toilet. At first I thought she was bluffing or up to some tricks. Most of all, when we were romancing nicely under the roof of her solitary confine. Back of my head, I knew that she was bloody running away from my romance. I decided to let her go. Isn't true that there are things that you have to let them go in order to watch them come back? So like a bird, I had to let her go and relieve herself or something like unto it. I stayed behind staring at the walls of silence that were somehow trying to capture the rage and violence of my penis.

Chapter Fifteen

Jorissen Place #66 is my favorite Braamfontein building, which is adjacent to University Corner and opposite Braamfontein Centre. What a beautiful building. I wonder who owns it? What type of activities takes place there? The facade is splendid and it is forever clean. It is huge. It occupies the whole block back-to-back by itself. Who was the architect? When was it built? I like its brownish-yellowish-cremish marble stone facade. Its granite finishes are outstanding- built to last.
Out of all the buildings in Braamfontein, #66 Jorissen place is my number one. Imagine me having my office there or converting one into a loft or a penthouse! I would be living a King's life in the middle of my favorite city, Braamfontein. By then, I would probably be not into women and sticking. Fuck it, I'm lying. 'Till I die I'll be game related. I love women and pussy like cats love milk and sleeping. If I can get it twice or thrice a day like it was my meals, it would be well with me. Anyway, I am not talking about them females; I am talking about my favorite Braamfontein building, #66 Jorissen Place. I don't even want to include information on who built or designed this perfectly built and perfectly situated building. When you read this text and you happen to be a lover of art and architecture and you love my city, Braamfontein- then you must research the information about this magnificent building.

I tell you, when this Braamfontein city is no more, one day, some day - #66 Jorissen Place will still be standing just like the temple of Solomon, just like the Rhodes Memorial, just like the Voortrekker

Monument, just like the Pyramids of Giza, just like the temples of the Aztecs and just like the Zimbabwe Ruins. #66 Jorissen Place is a monument in its own right, a force to be reckoned with, a masterpiece, a gem, and a mainstay. #66 Jorissen Place illuminates the light on the dark Braamfontein landscape.

She came back from the toilet and my erection was still performing. Gabaza was a nice pretty female but with low self-esteem, and that was beating me because how can a low self-esteem thing challenge me? So I had to think of ways to win my way to that sweet thing between her legs. Without hesitating, I grabbed her and laid her on her bed, and I started kissing and caressing her. This time around I was acting manly and not punkish (bitch-made). You act like a punk and no fucking for you. Weaklings never get what they want but what they are given. So I grabbed the female bull by its horns and I wrestled. Her floral dress was somewhere by her chest. Next thing I saw, I was fiddling with her sex organ and it was dripping wet. What happened next is something I didn't see coming. My thing was inside her warm thing, what a feeling! Warm, wet and slippery. It didn't take long and next thing that happened is that I was pissing the fluid on her; I couldn't hold it any longer. When I was finished releasing the fluid- reality hit me so bad that I quickly jumped out but to no avail because damage was already done. Damn- few minutes (in my case, few seconds) of pleasure result in lifetime of pain. I don't want to think negative but what if she gets pregnant? What the fuck am I thinking, she has to get pregnant if you stick your thing in her thing and release fluid while at it. It is natural. The question should be, are you ready and is she prepared to have a baby (fall pregnant)? You answer that when you are on top of your woman and hitting it *nyama*-to-*nyama*. What if she has AIDS?

What if she has some STD's? What if? What if? What if? Sticking can be bullshit if you're not careful. Maybe sticking was mainly meant for making babies and not for pleasure and leisure. I fucking didn't wear a condom when I was sticking Gabaza. How was I going to get time to put that rubber on when she was constantly fighting me? I had to trick her. Maybe it is time these females stop fighting us before we do it so that we can have a chance to get strapped without having to trick them. That shit is risky. Days later I heard on the news that Hazyview was sick with a high HIV+/AIDS rate. You can imagine how I felt subsequent to hearing that?

I was taking multivitamin pills every day, exercising every other day and eating healthy but other than that - I was keeping my head cool so I can boost my will power. Anyway, *zibhajwa kweziwudlayo*. I believe that the whole AIDS matter hits you hard when your will power is weak. It is all in your head. Do and try everything to keep your will power at its maximum peak in order to live long and achieve your destiny.

A mind (will power) is a terrible thing to waste, so don't even try. Better yet, use a condom if you can't abstain, I repeat.

The moment I got off of Gabaza still in my half-naked state, I was already feeling sick because my mind was already on frenzy and I was imagining all the worse that can happen.

Maybe she was imagining more worse than me for her sake like what if I get AIDS or fall pregnant from this irresponsible punk? Whatever it was, I didn't care- I was deep in my sorrowful-thinking state. I was saying or I kept saying to myself: "Never no more will I subject myself to such brutality and slow poison." Some of us only learn through sad experience, unfortunately. My mind was seriously playing tricks on me by now and I was seeing my dick shrinks and withers every second I looked at it. Same spot where there is joy pain is felt. I must have sat there on that bed for five minutes or so before I gained courage to wear my boxer shorts and jeans. Imagine coming into a place feeling high, good and shit and to leaving the same place feeling low, bad and shit?

A seriously fucked up feeling. I managed to crawl out of my solitary confinement and met Gabaza by the passage and I asked where the toilet was and she showed me. When I came back from the toilet she was fixing her bed (slaughtering table). I tried to spark a conversation but it was an empty one. She never questioned me about why I didn't use a condom but I thought maybe where she comes from she doesn't have a liberty to question man on such issues. I don't know but I needed something, some medicine to boost a will, which was weak. So I shifted the conversation as I internally consoled myself, by saying or by thinking that maybe she was healthy and is on the pill or loop or injection. I said to myself, if ever there were a next time, I would never subject myself to such nonsense. It is suicidal.

How can something so good be so deadly? I just don't understand! I tell you, for the next coming months and years, I always looked for her to see if she wasn't pregnant or had lost weight or something. Months went pass, years went pass and I never saw anything suspicious. I bumped into her four years after our "flirt with danger" stint and she never said anything that was alarming. It took me over four years to finally come down from my high state of alert. What for? For the sake of sticking we rather risk it all. Gabaza and me!

I'll be lying if I said I didn't hit it raw after that.

The reason why I won't go test for the traces of positivity of that pandemic disease, is because worrying will get me to the grave quicker than the sickness would. So mind can cure you and kill you. You start worrying because you know you are going to die soon. Ignorance is bliss! What I don't know won't kill me. I'm not rejoicing in ignorance but for manmade diseases such as AIDS that depends on your will power to survive them, not knowing will get you living longer than expected. They are busy forcing us to go testing, what for?

So they can make money out of our misery? Bloody cockroaches cloaked in suits, they are. Where there is a will there is a way.

Chapter Fifteen

Out of all the things that are foreign to an African or Bantu is this thing. This thing of sharing same bed or bedroom with your woman kills the excitement of sticking. Let me break it down for you: I believe that testosterone doesn't fully (completely) get along with oestrogen especially on a day-today basis. I believe that these two distinct hormones or energies must come together to serve a specific purpose(s) only, which is intercourse. Both energies are very independent and interdependency only happens when natural phenomenons are due. When male energy and female energy comes together, nirvana takes place, only for that period only and not for everyday all day. When purpose(s) have been fulfilled, these energies must separate to allow nature to deal with after-effects. To cool off. So then, why do men and women feel that they have to be always in each other's space all the time? They don't trust each other? Such behavior surely does cause mistrust because when one party starts following his or her inclinations, the fake bond is challenged. Take for example a man that is living-in with his women. Before sex the build up is exciting, during sex it is still exciting but the moment climax (orgasm) is reached, excitement evaporates into thin air. Man doesn't want to "cuddle" or be warm to the woman. At this point in time the man wish she can go away and give himself some fresh air (buenos aires). By now, she irritates him. Even worse when she says she wants some more when you have just cum, he roughs her up and say: "But I've just ejaculated, you gonna have to wait till my dick is up again. I'm not a robot."

That is why I am not a supporter of these living-in arrangements nor the same bed or bedroom-sharing order.

Another arrangement I'm struggling to comprehend or overcome is this one of sex before marriage. If you start "test driving" before marriage, won't that kill "romance" and "sex" once you're married? What is the rush? Can't you wait and practice onanism in the meantime? Or non-penetrative sex? Or abstain? I don't know how I feel about this one myself but something tells me that a lot of things can be prevented other than being cured. Sex is good. I love sex. I can't live without sex. I don't believe that having it all the time is a good thing; sometimes you have to miss it or have other things to keep yourself busy with. We can't live our daily lives bent on pleasures of sex. Sex is beautiful. For me, oral sex is better than intercourse. Though I don't believe that it was meant for that. Beauty in the hideous, hhe?

But back to the living-in arrangement, what causes these too much and unnecessary fighting and arguments? It is the sharing of one and the same space by the oestrogen figure and the testosterone figure. They argue over petty and bullshit issues that could have been avoided if one figure kept space from the other. You got to let people be, don't overcrowd them. This whole romantic gospel is misleading. They say you got to cuddle up on the couch and watch television. Such nonsense is good for them in Europe where it is mostly cold, not in Africa- it's hot down here so sister just give me space to stay cool. They say you got to sleep on the same bed. They say your friends must be her friends also.

Bullshit! Just let me be. You're sleeping and you

feeling hot, it's middle of summer and you want to open up windows for some breeze, you have stepped on a snake's tail.

"I'm cold, please close the windows."

"Add in an extra duvet or blanket."

"Don't be inconsiderate."

"I'm not, it's hot."

"You're being unfair and self-serving."

"I'm going to the other room, so relax. I'll close the windows for you my "queen". Do you want me to turn on the heater while I'm still at it?"

That fuckin nonsense pisses me off. For how long will I take such nonsense or for how long will I subject myself to such torment and lunacy?

That is why I say a man should have his room and the woman, her room. If she is a queen, why then is she sharing a bed?

Queens have their own beds and rooms. I am advocating and supporting such a move.

These living arrangements don't work for Blacks and they will never work. Such arrangements promote being effeminate, always understanding, a penis-less man, and easily persuaded and always agreeable man. Men- get your penises back, please, before it is too late.

If their definition of being romantic is going shopping with your woman, I say do it and let us see how long that will last. If their definition of being romantic is sleeping on the same bed and bedroom with your woman, I say do it and see how long it is going to last before you are castrated of your God-given manly powers of decision making and being firm.

I guess it becometh for every man to do right by

him and his.

But either way, men must not betray their manliness and get carried away by what these magazines and these and those experts say about how to live our lives and to take care of our loved ones. But tell me, where did we go wrong and loose it that now we have to be told how to socialize with our fellow mankind? Slavery? Colonialism? Apartheid?

Post colonialism? Neocolonialism? What? I guess we will never know. But just in on the issue of living-in arrangements, let us not curse our future babies while we at it. A nice movie I watched the other day titled *MAAR* WHY?, Depicts well these dynamics of the Black middle class in the "post-Apartheid" South Africa (era). A beautiful movie, I recommend it. Every Black men and women must watch *MAAR* WHY?.

Chapter Sixteen

I was arguing with this other *umfazi* (woman with sexual experience) on the phone the other day about the difference between males and females. So I started talking shit (just to irritate her) about how long in a year it will take a man to make babies compared to how long it would take a female. So I started asking her a bunch of questions. Why does a woman once a month or so she gets her periods when her egg (ovum) is not fertilized? Does that mean that the egg expires and she has to bleed for not making use of it timely? Why does she suffer so much pain when she menstruates? Why when she has a baby the pain lessens? If she gets a baby every year will she experience such pain often? Before she reaches menopause she is suppose to be making babies? Only those men that can control (rule) women can be polygamous, not penis-less men. Those need to grow their penises back first. She didn't have a comment or an opinion, she just said: "Bye" and hung up.

A funny thing happened the other day. Okay, let me tell you a story about this female that I once messed with a while back.

I am reminded of her story because I have recently seen her gyrating on some House music video on television. She was a tall, dark and thick lady. Very stylish indeed. I met her one time; she was walking around Braamfontein by Long Bar. I tapped her on her shoulder like Mr. Cheeks did to Renee. She said her name was, ehh? I forgot her name. From that day on I kept in touch with my Venda one. She was from Limpopo, somewhere in Limpopo. Why does it seem that almost every woman that lives in Braamfontein is from Limpopo? 65% of these women tell you that they are from that interesting province. I love Limpopo, the terrain, their fruits and veggies and to top it all - their women. They are beautiful, loving and giving. You don't have to give much to get more from one. They understand even if they don't understand.

Though I must admit, most of them get released (unleashed) to the streets of Johannesburg no longer virgins and/or innocent. These future mother's of our children go loose in the city and when exhausted go back home and marry an unsuspecting man. Fuck, who cares? Johannesburg lost its innocence the day it was born, probably even when it was being conceived. So who am I to pass unrighteous judgment on these beautiful women by saying they are loose when the city is also loose? The city is like a mother of all broads.

Johannesburg is a mother to Braamfontein. Besides, I'm not going to act like "holier than thou" when I am also a recipient of the degeneracy that is produced in masses by the city. That is why I love the city - it is loose, no morals, all you need to survive in this place is money, there is no love, we live for the moment, it never rests, it is no place like home and it is cold and calculating.

Back to my Venda dark-beauty. She invited me over her place one time and I agreed. She stayed in Melridge, one of the abundantly many student residences in Braamfontein. I arrived on time and ready for whatever. I buzzed her when I was downstairs. My dick was already pounding and bulging- excited at the prospect of getting a fresh meal. After five minutes, she came down with her round eyes, and she was dark and beautiful. We stood outside the building just chatting and trying to get my mind right and my words right on what to say to get her to take me up to her room so I can give her a sample (stick her). I am all about sticking, stick, stick stick, that's what I am about man! I like it like I like junk food.

When I finally got to make my intentions known, she quickly responded by telling me that her friend was by her room so she can't go up to the room with me. I asked her to repeat herself and she did. I was pissed. Come on now, who gets ready for war and gets with his enemy and the enemy tells him: "We won't fight today. I'll pick another day for our war." Rules of battle - engagement don't go that way. War is war. So yeah, I was disappointed. I walked away from her with my tail tugged neatly between my legs. I think I just went for a beer or something or I just went and ran a thing or two in Braamfontein. My pounding erection was highly disappointed.

To cut a long story short, I arranged for another meeting during the day. It must have been a week or two later. My Venda one came down to sign me in. She was looking all nice and stuff. At first I thought she was expecting to go some where with me because of the way she was dressed. She was dressed to parade town. But anyway, these females are always nicely dressed even if they are going nowhere in particular.

This woman was nice, as I have hinted before. She was thick, dark and beautiful. I love dark skins and light skins. I love the ass, the bigger the better. I am a sucker for ass, you understand? I don't understand these Black females who have no ass, where were they when the Ass Truck was distributing thick asses around the township? Maybe they had already moved to the suburbs. Don't they know that Black is the new thing nowadays? Being Black is the in thing. Even Whites want to be Black!

Anyway, I'm up in her room, right? No one else was in the room so it was all smooth sailing. The fucked up thing is that I didn't come prepared. I didn't have condoms. I was caught unprepared because I thought that she wouldn't let me stick her. So I relaxed and let down my guard. Technically, I fucked myself, I went to war with my enemy thinking there would be peaceful talks and a truce but I was wrong, my enemy was ready for sticking and she wanted to get me fucked or she thought I was ready for sticking - I came unprepared for sticking. Never underestimate your opponent, you must always come prepared or don't come at all. What was I thinking?

Honestly, it's time these females keep condoms incase we forget to bring them. It's shit like this that makes us stick without.

We were kissing and rubbing nice and shit. I got her undressed - strip naked and she was reciprocal. Damn, why didn't I bring my condom(s)?

"Do you have condoms?"

I asked a rhetorical question and its answer was horrible. Imagine me saying that let's go to the shops to buy condoms, which would have been insane. It would have been like aborting a good mission. I calmed myself down and opted for oral sex, which to me is better than intercourse. Though sometimes a man needs to release the overflowing semen bubbling somewhere inside the scrotum.

Having my dick sucked is like heaven. She went down and started sucking and nibbling on my shit. It was nice, very nice. She put me under pressure, so now I'm feeling like, I gotta return the favor, so we switched positions. While she was sucking me I was licking her vagina juices, the tasteless juices, the juices that drips down your moustache. Honestly, I really stooped low, so low because I had long told myself that I would never go down and lick their wounds. They must suck my roll-on. Anyway, we was busy doing the nasty and I was busy licking her shit with my eyes closed, afraid that my eyes might stray and see her big black shit-crusted ass. It is things such as these that your mother or grandmother used to say: "*Ungang'buki ng'chama, uzovalek' amehlo.*" I never did anyway, look at me now, I'm under this big black blonde's shitty crotch area. Some stuff that can really make you go blind. So through out the process my eyes were closed, the problem was that I had gas, lot of gas on my stomach and it was rushing down my colon to come out. While she was busy sucking, I couldn't hold it any longer, so I farted on that woman's face.

Chapter Seventeen

The way Braamfontein is so quiet it worries me because I always get a feeling that there is spiritual wickedness going on the surface and underneath the surface. I would like to believe that the drug problem (substance abuse) is part of what is keeping the city ticking (Tik-ing). Most of the drug mules are residing in this city. I know a particular one, myself. Open your eyes and look around. Don't sleepwalk in this city where things take shape every single second, minute and hour. I love my city. I hate my city.

Braamfontein women are cheaper than poor Hillbrow or Yeoville or Bez-Valley prostitutes. A dumpy or two of Storm or Savannah or Sarita - you are sticking. You just buy once and the second time you're sticking for free. You have unlocked the path and gates to her ready to yield legs (pussy). A way to the hearts of these Braamfontein women is through their legs. What is this place coming to? Where in the world have you heard of police shooting soldiers? The Bheki Cele orders are making these police go shooting our national security. If Zimbabwe or Namibia were to attack us today, which battalion will defend our nation?

Omantindane who can't function independently without being instructed and commanded in all things. Slothful servants.

How dare do they embarrass the men that are trained for mortal combat? How do you do such? It's insane. The soldiers are now pissed and they want payback. Anarchy around the door, I smell it. Zuma-WATCH OUT! These guys are going to depose you as soon as they seat you. Don't let us to be like Nigeria and the likes where military dictators do people worse than Idi Amin did his Ugandans. Anyone can be touched, no one is invisible or is superman. *"Inkosi yinkosi" ngabantu bayo.* How you gonna call yourself government when your ways of governing us are as fucked as a group of stupid men that rape a two year old baby? God and the gods allowed you to be our prime minister so don't go taking advantage of us and what you have been entrusted with. MR. PRESIDENT: suffer us not to be led into temptation! We are willing to support you and make our country a better place.

Mr. Zuma: I don't ever want my country to go to the hands of the White Man again. I don't want it to go to the hands of the Indian Man, China Man or others. They have their own countries where they can do as they please. It's bad enough as it is that the foreigners enjoy my country more than I do and yet I can't enjoy their country. They get the best of both worlds and me I get hell. Mr. President, how long will that go for?

Something must be done quick quick in order to win the trust and love of those men and women that got humiliated by the police the other day. Please, somebody, give them what they want otherwise they are going to refuse to go defend our country, the country of our forefathers. When such happens, we would be on our own, and we can't expect police to defend the nation, they were not trained for such. Police are like security guards; they can't even fire an AK-47. They can't drive a tank. They can't fly a chopper. They can't even make a Molotov cocktail. Let alone surviving harsh terrain for a month and more. Have you seen how fat these cops are? Some are even obese. Then, you are going to expect them to defend you, lay down their lives for the sake of yours? Look at their asses, they are fat cats, lazy as fuck. All they do is take bribes, kill each other, be corrupt, and shoot to kill our brothers and friends. Police are only good when it comes to protecting the estate and interests of their masters, the State. They are the agents of the State. The dogs of the State. I don't like them police.

Maybe I will like them if they became the agents of the people, served and protected us from the criminals, thieves, robbers and murderers. Protected our interests and livelihoods. Maybe then, only then I'll say: God bless the police.

They shoot us for no apparent reason; we shoot back with apparent reason. This is not the Wild West. This is not New York City or any other place like unto it where Blacks get shot and killed and police say it was a mistake. We must sue them if they think they are going to shoot at us like they were target practicing. Bullshit! Look at what they did to Amadou Diallo? Look at what they did to Sean Bell? Who shot Biggie Smalls? Who shot Tupac Shakur? Who shot Lucky Dube? They'll be shooting and killing us every night and day. Oh, it's the police, trigger-itchy finger police. They are trained to serve and protect the selective few.

Chapter Eighteen

How my Krugersdorp thing and me ended is like this. She invited me to her work. She worked at a funeral parlor.

Doves to be exact. The first time I asked her where she works she told me that it was just up the road on Jorissen Street.

I never really cared much about enquiring the specifics. When she told me that she works for Doves, my heart sank. It just went cold. I tried to toughen up so I can keep my appointment with her. I got to admit, I don't like being in the company of the dead.

I buzzed her when I was outside Doves and she came out. We went to her office at the back and she was explaining to me what it is that she does. She organizes funeral events such as booking and coordinating church services, organizing tombstone matters as well as other matters related to the dead. The interest, excitement and erections I have been entertaining every time I would think of her - they jumped out the window. But tell me, who in the right mind would run game, let me put this nicely. Who in the hell will go see (check) his ladyfriend at a funeral parlor? That shit is fucked up. You are in the company of the dead and yet you are romancing the idea of sticking. I just couldn't deal with that psychosis. I left, instigated a fight (argument) two days later, deleted her numbers and I was out. No more.

If I were to mention all the things I've stuck in Braamfontein I will never finish this text.

Like all good things, they always come to an end. I have had a fair share of sticking at Shawshank, too numerous to number and list down. Most of it was junk sex like fast food that you eat and get full but still feel hungry. It didn't take long before I got myself kicked out of Shawshank for sticking more things there than the guys who actually lived there. I came to find out that the storm had been brewing ever since; they were just waiting for the right time to dispose me accordingly. They say that one must watch his Kaffirs because they can and do act worse than bitches.

They are skimming, conniving, plotting and backstabbing.

Biggie Smalls said: "Who is it? It's the ones that smoked blunts with you, they see your picture and now they grab the guns to come and get you." It's true, your friends "can be your worse enemies, they know your ins and outs and they act like bitches." Just like my big ass ex-ladyfriend used to say: "Punk, bitch-ass nigga." I miss that big ass one. When I provoked her and she gets pissed, she would say that.

One day we were at Shawshank drinking, the usual. I went to buy some food to be cooked, with Lava. We came back cooked it and ate just when we were about to finish, in comes Jika and starts throwing in some tantrums like a little spoiled brat.

He starts complaining that I am finishing their food, always using their beds to fuck my never-ending hordes of whores, and never thanking them for it. Wow, jealousy is a motherfucker. All along them brothers have or were harboring such feelings! I remember that I had a piece of *boerewors* I was chewing in my mouth but for some strange reason my throat had a sudden warm feeling and every time I tried to push down the meat through my epiglottis, it just wouldn't go down. So I spat it out on my plate and dumped the plate on the floor.

Jika was now joined by Lava as they rained down their grievances on me and to some other guys that were there with me that they knew as well. Jika kept saying that I am always reducing his bed mileage- meaning that he never stick any things on his bed and since he bought it, I have fucked more things in it than him as the owner of the bed. Remember that alcohol was in the mix of all this bitch-talk that was going on, so I decided to fight back and I was telling them shit, especially Jika, punk-bitch. Lava, I taught him or reminded him that he was spineless and had no balls, a typical emasculated specimen. He can't stand up for his own decisions or speak out his mind. These guys are weaker than my weak erection. Featherweights. I told him that he must stand up for himself in all that he says or does. Jika? I told him that he was a coward, a jerk and a looser with low self-esteem.

A grown man with pimples all over his face, how fucked up is that? He needs an enema and a purgative to clean his bad blood.

Jika slept on a passage, his bed was by the lounge, which was partitioned by a room-divider (bookshelf) to separate it from the "living-room" area. Jika was afraid of women, he always inherited my leftovers. Some woman I wanted a while back, I found out that he was busy warming her up and backstabbing me. What a bloody snake! Worse than a snake. The other homeboys were dissing them too, I wasn't the only one.

Besides, Jika and Lava were disrespecting all of us and were we to take such insults with a smile? Fuck that, I ain't no punk - got to fight back when I'm being challenged. Wrong or right - you got to fight for what is rightfully yours. This time I was fighting for my dignity, self-respect and pride since it was being trampled upon by people I regarded as "friends." I knew I was way better than those guys, they just couldn't handle me, compete with me, or outdo me. I was too much for them, that's what they said. I embarrassed them and made them look like weaklings in their own section. When they finally developed balls and grew their penises a bit, they decided to call me into order. Nonsense - I called them into order right at their own place. What kind of guys is going to cry over a tin of baked beans and maize meal for pap? They worse than females, matter of fact; they are females – double gendered species (hermaphrodites). They cry over food like garbage hungries. To think that I had homeboys like these was crazy; I was disillusioned, thinking that we were boys whereas all along I was in the company of whores that suffer from verbal diarrhea. Anyway, *okungapheli kuyahlola* and good things always come to an end. I should have given them some tampons; they were on their periods.

The dog in me makes me feel for the lust. My double standard ness makes me a victim and a victimizer in this city so degenerated. A city that hardly sleeps depends on junk, fast food. Fast cars, fast life, fast money, fast sex, fast love, short attention spans and short tempers. Truth be told, I love my city more than I hate my city. I don't own it but allow me to claim it. Some Whites in Stellenbosch own it or some

Americans or some Brits somewhere, run the city. Braamfontein, if the Bezuidenhouts were to resurrect today and see what their farm had become, they would fall down and die again. So much decay. Just like our morals, Braamfontein needs some regeneration.